# The Lunchbox Mystery

## Alison Lohans

Illustrations by Janet Wilson

SCHOLASTIC CANADA INC.

*To John, with love from Mom*

**Canadian Cataloguing in Publication Data**

Lohans, Alison, 1949-
   The lunchbox mystery

Previously published under title: Mystery of the lunchbox criminal.
ISBN 1-55268-557-8

I. Wilson, Janet, 1952-  . II. Title. III. Title: Mystery of the lunchbox criminal.

PS8573.O35M98 1999          jC813'.54          C98-932791-4
PZ7.L65Lu 1999

Copyright © 1990, 1999 by Alison Lohans.

5 4 3 2 1          Printed and bound in Canada          9/9 0 1 2 3/0

# Contents

# Surprise!

"**I**'m *hungry!*" said J.J. "I'm so hungry I could eat a house."

"Huh," said Derek. "What about the windows? You'd chew up the glass, and then you'd bleed and you'd —"

"Oh, be quiet," J.J. said. His stomach was growling and it was only recess. He knew there were three pieces of ham and pineapple pizza in his lunchbox. "Just wait till you see my lunch," he said. "It's *awesome.*"

"Huh," said Derek. "All you can think about is food. The bell's going to ring and we still have to race our cars."

"There's time," J.J. said. He wasn't sure about racing his remote control Z-28 in the school yard. Derek liked to crash cars. And what if that bully Shaun Higgins saw them and took the Z-28 away? Or stepped on it.

"Hurry up!" said Derek. "You're wasting our whole recess. Maybe I'll race Kyle instead."

"All right!" said J.J. "I'm ready." He traced a line in the dirt. "We'll go from here to the monkey bars. OK?"

J.J. didn't want Derek to race Kyle King. Kyle was friends with Shaun. And sometimes he acted just as mean.

"Go!" Derek yelled.

J.J. pressed the button and watched his car go. Be careful of the rock, he thought. Oops! He hadn't noticed that twig and he'd run right over it. He was off course. Derek was winning!

The bell rang. J.J. scooped up his car. "Race you to the door," he said.

"Huh. Who wants to race *you?*" Derek said. "All you do is waste time talking about food."

J.J. ran anyway.

His stomach growled all morning. Once it growled so loudly that the whole class laughed. Miss Davis smiled at him. "Ready for lunch already, J.J.?" she asked.

J.J. felt his face getting hot. "I guess so," he said.

He'd only had five cornflakes for breakfast. He would have had more, but his baby sister Jessica knocked his bowl onto the floor. And there wasn't a single flake left in the box. Dad was out of town at a conference, so breakfast was late to start with. Then Mom got an important long-distance phone call. Nobody noticed the toast was stuck in the toaster until the kitchen was filled with smoke. And by that time, J.J. had to leave for school.

He thought of the pizza in his lunchbox. Mom had ordered an extra large yesterday, so they had lots of leftovers.

"J.J." Was that the second time Miss Davis had said his name?

"Sorry," he said. "I didn't hear you."

"For the third time, J.J., how do you spell *piano?*"

"*P-I-Z-Z-A,*" he spelled loudly. His mouth watered at the thought. And then, when the class laughed again, he realized his mistake.

Tanya Webster was waving her hand in the air. "Miss Davis? I know it, Miss Davis. *P-I-A-N-O.*"

"Showoff," J.J. said to himself. He checked his watch — 11:30. Then he looked at the clock on the wall. It said 11:28. How could he possibly wait all that time until lunch? He might starve to death by then! Would his body stay sitting in his desk, he wondered, or would it fall down in the aisle? Maybe there would be a fire drill and they would get to go to lunch earlier than usual.

No such luck. The class had to copy each spelling word one more time in their notebooks. And then J.J. had to stay after, because instead of writing *piano*, he'd spelled *pizza* again.

The lunch room was noisy when he walked in. He had to look hard to find Derek. And then he had to walk past Shaun and Kyle to get there. Shaun stuck his foot out and J.J. saw it too late. He tripped. His lunchbox went flying with a clatter. The latches opened. His thermos rolled off in one direction. The rest of his lunch . . . where *was* the rest of his lunch? Where was his pizza?

"*What?*" cried J.J. "Where's my lunch? Where's my pizza?"

Shaun started laughing. So did Kyle.

J.J. turned to the bully. "Where's my pizza?" he asked. "I bet you took it."

"Did not." Shaun opened his mouth wide. It smelled like peanut butter. There was even peanut butter stuck on his teeth.

"He never touched your lunch," Kyle agreed. "I was with him all morning."

J.J. blinked fast and took a deep breath. Had Kyle taken his pizza? He didn't dare blame these two if he didn't have proof. "It's not fair," he said under his breath.
"I was so hungry! It's not *fair!*" He turned away and wiped his eyes with his arm.

"Here, J.J." Tanya Webster was holding out half a sandwich. "You can have this."

"But I want my pizza!" J.J. said.

Finally Mr. Muller noticed. "What's going on here?" he asked. "Shaun Higgins, what have you done this time?"

"I never —"

J.J. said, "Somebody stole my pizza. What am I going to eat? I'm starving!"

Derek crawled under a table and came back with J.J.'s thermos.

J.J. grabbed it. "Leave my stuff alone!"

The lunch room was very quiet. "We're going to get to the bottom of this," Mr. Muller said. "Whoever took J.J.'s lunch should be ashamed. How would you feel if you had your food stolen? Somebody owes J.J. an apology and a lunch."

Mr. Muller was only trying to help, but J.J.'s face got hot again. He sneaked a look at Shaun and Kyle. Mr. Muller was glaring at them and they were glaring at J.J. They would be waiting for him after school.

Meanwhile, Ginny Chen had given him some chips, Lisa French had shared her celery sticks and somebody had put three chocolate chip oatmeal cookies at his place. He wouldn't go hungry after all — today. But what if the same thing happened again tomorrow? Or the next day?

"I'm going to get to the bottom of this," J.J. said to himself.

# More Problems

By the end of the day J.J. was feeling better. In gym he'd been the last one caught in the dodgeball game. And he'd gotten the best mark in class on his social studies test. But Derek was beginning to get on his nerves.

"I bet your mom didn't even fix you a lunch," Derek said as they walked along. It was the third time he'd said it since they left school. This time he even laughed.

J.J. was beginning to wish Derek would get lost — except then he'd be all alone if he met Shaun and Kyle. "I told you a million zillion times!" he burst out. "She did! She gave me pizza for lunch!"

"Did you see her?" asked Derek.

"No," J.J. said. "But she'd never give me an empty lunchbox."

"Nobody's mom would do that," said Tanya Webster. She and her little sister Amy had been tagging along behind them. "That's too mean."

"You never know," said Derek.

"What kind of friend are you?" said J.J. "Get lost!"

Derek gave a rock a big kick. It went across the street and down an alley. So did Derek.

At first J.J. was happy. Leaving Amy and Tanya behind, he dodged from side to side along the sidewalk. That's how he'd won the dodgeball game.

Then he started thinking about Shaun and Kyle. Without Derek around, it would be two against one and he might end up with a bloody nose. Then Mom would get all upset because he'd been fighting. But J.J. hadn't seen Shaun or Kyle since the bell rang. Maybe they *had* stolen his lunch. Maybe Mr. Muller had sent them to see Mrs. Markoski, the principal.

How could J.J. keep the same thing from happening tomorrow? And if it did, would his mom pick him up and take him for hamburgers or something? Probably not. Jessica took up whatever time Mom had left over from studying.

J.J. was almost home when something hard cracked him on the head. "*Ow!*" he yelled. He touched the spot on his head. A lump was already beginning to grow.

Not too far away, he heard laughing. He opened his eyes and saw Shaun standing behind a parked car. Was Kyle there too? He couldn't tell. J.J. took a deep breath and started to run. He could hear footsteps pounding behind him. Then there was a yell. It sounded like a karate yell.

J.J. turned to look. Tanya Webster was facing Shaun. She moved so quickly that J.J. couldn't tell what she did. But Shaun went flying through the air and landed hard.

"I saw what you did, Shaun Higgins," she shouted. "You're so mean it makes me sick!"

"Huh?" Derek had appeared from somewhere. He stood there staring.

"Look out!" J.J. yelled as Shaun picked up another rock.

"Don't try it," Tanya said. "I'm almost up to black belt, you know."

"You couldn't be," Shaun said. "You're a girl."

"Want to find out?" she asked.

Shaun made an ugly face at her. When Tanya began moving toward him, he dropped the rock.

"Hey! You kids!" somebody yelled. "Quit that fighting!"

J.J. looked down the street. It was Mrs. Peterson. She was big and so was her voice.

For sure, when Mrs. Peterson said something, everybody listened.

"We were just having a little fun," said Shaun.

"Some fun," said J.J.

"Shoo!" said Mrs. Peterson. "We don't need any rocks thrown here, thank you. I'll be very happy to let your parents know about this."

"I was just leaving anyway," Shaun said.

J.J. looked at Tanya. He was still surprised by what he'd seen.

"See you later," Tanya said with a wave.

Derek just stood there staring.

When J.J. got home, the car wasn't in the driveway and the door was locked. "Figures," he said. He dropped down on the front steps to wait. He couldn't help feeling mad at his mom. She didn't seem to care much about him anymore. All she ever did was study and look after Jessica. He touched the lump on his head. Ow!

Finally, the car rolled into the driveway. "You're late," J.J. said as his mother got the baby out of her car seat. "It's after 4:30."

"I'm sorry, J.J.," his mom said with a tired smile. "I had to take Jessica to the doctor and we had a long wait." She gave him a quick hug. "I'm sorry you had to wait outside all this time." Then she noticed him touching his head. "What happened?" She felt the lump. "Have you been fighting?"

"Shaun hit me with a rock," he said.

His mom's mouth went into an angry line.

"Aren't you going to say anything?" J.J. demanded. "I got hit in the head with a rock. Don't you even care? I bet you don't care about my lunch either." He stomped up the front steps.

"J.J.!" Mom said sharply. "Just give me a minute to get Jessica inside. She has a fever and I need to put her to bed. Then we'll talk about it. All right?"

Jessica started crying.

"Oh, boy," said J.J. He covered his ears. He felt like kicking the door, but decided he'd better not. When they got inside, he looked at his watch. One minute passed. "OK," he said. "A minute's up."

"J.J.!" Mom yelled. "I won't have you behaving like this. Go to your room until I call you."

J.J. pounded up the stairs. He made sure it was good and loud so Mom would hear. The whole day had been a disaster, and all she had time for was the baby. And her books.

Well, maybe one thing hadn't been a disaster. It had been pretty neat when Tanya sent Shaun flying. He wished he could see her do it again. Maybe he could talk Mom into letting him learn karate too.

At last his mom knocked on his door. "J.J.?" she said softly.

"What?" He was lying on his stomach on his bed.

His mom came in and sat beside him. "I'm

sorry about all the trouble you had after school," she said. "We'd better figure out a safe place to keep a key so you can let yourself in."

"I need a safe place to keep my lunch too."

"How was the pizza?" asked Mom.

"There *wasn't* any pizza!" J.J. yelled. "And you don't even care!"

"What?" said Mom. "What happened to the pizza I packed?"

"It was gone," J.J. told her angrily. "Shaun tripped me and my lunchbox fell and spilled. All that came out was my thermos."

Mom rubbed her forehead. "But how could that be? What did you have to eat?"

J.J. told her. He knew she wasn't the guilty person. He'd just have to catch the criminal. No way he was having his lunch stolen again.

# Criminal at Work

At morning recess the next day, J.J. and Derek ran to the far corner of the playground behind the concrete tunnels.

"Can you believe that Tanya Webster?" Derek said. "Threw Shaun down like a piece of cardboard!"

"Yeah!" J.J. agreed. "I wish I could do that!"

"Me too!" Derek's eyes sparkled.

J.J. checked over his shoulder to make sure nobody was listening. "I've got pizza for lunch again," he said. "And I taped my lunchbox shut. If anybody gets into it, I'll be able to tell."

"Huh," said Derek. "They could still take your pizza."

A cold feeling twisted in J.J.'s stomach. Derek was right. "Well anyway," he said, "it would be simpler to take a lunchbox that *wasn't* all taped shut. I thought about it all night. Whoever took my pizza probably did it at recess. Miss Davis is always in the room before school, but at recess she goes to the staff room."

"Are you going to waste our whole recess talking about your lunch again?" said Derek.

"But it could happen again!" J.J. said. "And it could happen to your lunch too. We've got to catch the criminal!"

"What criminal?" asked Derek.

J.J. wished Derek was more interested. "The Lunchbox Criminal!" he burst out. "We've got to catch him."

"Catch Shaun is more like it," said Derek. "And what makes you think I'd want to catch *him?*"

Derek had a point.

"Well . . ." J.J. thought for a minute. Then he remembered. "Shaun was outside all recess yesterday."

Derek wrinkled his forehead. "Huh. You're right."

"We should keep an eye on the classroom," J.J. said. He ran over and looked in a window. "Hey!" he cried. "Somebody's in there!"

"Where?" Derek pressed his nose against the glass. "What! Is that *my* lunchbox he's messing with?" He raced for the door.

J.J. stayed a moment longer to watch. But the person inside had heard their voices. He put the lunchbox back on the shelf and slipped out of the room.

J.J. crouched down. His heart was pounding. Think! he told himself. Who was it?

It hadn't been Shaun Higgins. In fact, he wasn't sure it was anybody he knew. All he'd seen was the criminal's back. He had light

brown hair, grey jogging pants and a dirty blue T-shirt. J.J. stood up and ran to catch up with Derek.

But Mr. Muller stopped him at the door. "What's the hurry, J.J.?" he asked. "The bell hasn't rung yet. You know the rules."

"But — but —" J.J. began. Where was Derek? He took a deep breath. "We saw somebody in the classroom. With the lunches."

"Oh!" Mr. Muller took off with quick steps. J.J. had to run to keep up.

They found Derek looking at his lunch. "Derek Scott!" Mr. Muller roared. "What are you doing in the classroom during recess?"

"No!" J.J. called. "Derek saw him too! Then he ran in and —"

"What are you doing, Derek?" asked Mr. Muller again.

"Checking my lunch," he said. "He didn't take anything."

No one in J.J.'s class had an empty lunchbox that day. But a girl from Mr.

Muller's room did. Mr. Muller frowned at J.J. and Derek.

"He thinks we had something to do with it!" J.J. said.

"You and your stupid ideas," Derek grumbled.

So far, today hadn't been much better than yesterday. But J.J. *had* seen somebody in the classroom. So had Derek. Somehow they'd have to catch that criminal — and prove it wasn't them!

# Another Detective

"I think we should forget about being detectives. If I get in trouble at school, I'll probably be grounded for a week," Derek said after school that day. The two boys were riding their skateboards down Cameron Street toward the river.

J.J. shook his head. "How can you talk about giving up? We saw the criminal. We almost caught him too!" He gave a good strong push. *Ka-chuk, ka-chuk, ka-chuk.* His wheels went over the cracks in the sidewalk like a train going down the tracks.

Tanya Webster was jumping rope just

ahead. So was her little sister Amy, but she kept tripping on her rope.

"Here I come!" yelled J.J. "Look out!"

"*You* look out," said Tanya. She didn't miss a skip.

J.J. rolled closer. "Here comes the famous lunchbox detective," he said. "Let him through in the name of the law!"

Tanya didn't move. Her chin stuck out. "Sidewalks are for people. You've got wheels, so you go in the street."

"Huh," said Derek. He kept coming too.

Tanya glared at the boys. J.J. dragged his toe on the sidewalk and stopped his skateboard. Derek did the same.

"Man, that was cool what you did to Shaun!" J.J. said. "I'm going to get my mom to let me take karate too."

"I'm already signed up," Derek boasted. J.J. had a feeling he was lying.

"Hey, Tanya," said J.J., "we saw the lunchbox criminal at work today."

Derek frowned. "And *we* got in trouble."

"You saw him?" Tanya said. "Who was it?"

"I don't know," said J.J. "I couldn't tell who it was. But it wasn't Shaun."

"I can jump rope," Amy said proudly.

J.J. sighed. Little sisters could be such a pain. Tanya seemed to think so too. "Who wants to jump rope?" she said. "Go play someplace else, Amy."

"Noooooo," whined Amy.

"I'll let you have three pieces of my bubble gum," Tanya said in an extra-nice voice.

Amy thought it over for a minute, and then said, "OK." She took the gum and skipped away.

"You saw him?" Tanya asked again in a low voice. "We'd better make plans to trap him!"

J.J. looked at Derek.

"Huh," said Derek. "Who said we want a girl to help?"

Tanya looked hurt.

"We need Tanya," J.J. said. "She has a special talent." He gave her a good hard look. "You'll help keep Shaun away?" he asked.

"I'll think about it," she said.

"OK. Come on. Let's go to the hideout," he said.

"*What?*" Derek yelled. "You'd give away our hideout?"

"We've got to work together," said J.J. "Tanya won't give away our secret." He gave her another hard look. "Will you?"

"Cross my heart and hope to die, stick a needle in my eye," she promised.

J.J. believed her. He aimed his skateboard and pushed off with his foot. "Away to catch the criminal!" he cried.

Derek followed and Tanya ran behind. She finally caught up with them at the river. "That's not fair!" she panted.

"Huh," said Derek. "So get yourself a skateboard."

Tanya's chin jutted out. "You just wait. I will!"

J.J. began climbing the steep grassy hill that had been built along the river to prevent flooding. "We'll be like real detectives," he said. "We'll look for clues and —"

But Derek wasn't listening. "Girls can't skateboard," he said as they ran downhill again toward a clump of willow trees.

"Who says?" demanded Tanya.

"I do," Derek said.

J.J. ducked into the narrow spot between the willow branches and the river bank. Just for a moment he was alone in a green world of leaves and branches. Here and there he could peek through and see the glint of water.

The green walls moved and Derek's head popped in, then Tanya's. Her eyes glowed as she followed Derek into the hideout. "This is great!" she whispered. "We can see out and nobody can see us!"

"That's the idea," J.J. said.

"Let's trap the criminal," Tanya went on. "You know, in the act."

"How?" asked Derek. He was crouching low beneath the branches.

"We'll fix it somehow so that anyone who moves a lunchbox will get caught. Let me think."

J.J. swatted at mosquitoes while Tanya sat thinking.

"Cans!" she shouted.

J.J. and Derek both jumped.

"Tin cans!" she said again.

"What are you talking about?" asked J.J.

Tanya explained her plan. It sounded as if it might work. They hoped the lunchbox criminal would strike again tomorrow.

# The Plan

During reading time next morning, the whole class went to the library. Miss Davis was talking to Mrs. Bourassa, the librarian. J.J. crossed his fingers for luck and said, "Miss Davis, I forgot my library book. Can I get it from my desk?"

She said yes and reminded him to be quiet in the hall. Then she turned to Kyle. He was bouncing his eraser off the globe.

J.J. darted out the back doors of the school. He and Tanya had hidden their backpacks in the bushes. J.J. held his nose and grabbed the smelly backpacks, then crept back inside.

Tanya came out of the girls' washroom. J.J. tried to hurry, but with every step the backpacks made a clanking noise.

"Shh!" Tanya hissed.

They tiptoed to the classroom. J.J. got his library book out of his desk, so he wouldn't be lying.

"Hurry!" said Tanya. "This has to work!"

J.J. unfastened the backpacks. With a clatter, empty cans tumbled out and rolled around on the floor. There were juice cans, sardine cans and dog food cans. A soup can had some eggshell stuck inside. A dribble of Coke spilled out of a pop can that Derek had found on the way to school.

"Yuck!" they both said at once.

J.J. moved a desk to the back of the room and climbed onto it so he could look inside the cupboard that was over the lunchbox shelf.

"Is there enough room?" Tanya asked. She was unwinding a ball of string.

"Just barely." J.J. jumped down. He started

tossing the cans into the plastic grocery bags Tanya had brought. It was Derek's job to keep the teacher busy — if Kyle didn't. But they didn't know how long they'd have before she noticed they hadn't come back to the library. Or before Kyle got in so much trouble that she decided to bring him back to the classroom.

"Hurry!" Tanya said again. With the string, she made a giant loop that ran through the handles of all the lunchboxes.

Footsteps sounded at the far end of the hall. *"Someone's coming!"*

As fast as he could, J.J. looped the handles of the grocery bags together with string. Then he tied one end of another long piece of string to his loop. He climbed back up on the desk and lifted the bags. Beneath him, Tanya was tying the other end of the long string to the loop that connected all the lunchboxes.

The footsteps kept coming closer . . .

J.J. stuffed the bags in the cupboard and pushed the door shut. When he jumped down, the door opened a little and a few cans rolled out and clattered to the floor. The sound was loud in the quiet room.

"What did you do that for?"

"It wasn't my fault!" J.J. said. "If you don't like the way I'm doing it, then do it yourself."

He picked the cans up and put them in his backpack. Then he shoved the desk back to its place. The footsteps came closer . . . and closer . . . and stopped!

J.J. sighed with relief. He picked up his library book. "Don't forget to cut the strings before lunch," he said.

Tanya nodded.

Miss Davis was looking at Derek's notebook when J.J. and Tanya went into the library. Derek's face was red. J.J. quietly put the library book in the return box and went to work.

When the class returned to the classroom, Miss Davis stopped and sniffed. "What's that funny smell?" she asked.

J.J.'s heart was beating so hard he was sure Miss Davis would hear it.

"I don't smell anything," Tanya said.

"*I* do," said Kyle. He made throwing-up noises.

"That's enough, Kyle," Miss Davis said. "Class, get out your science books."

J.J. grinned at Tanya and Derek. The trap was set!

But there was one thing they hadn't counted on. Ginny Chen came in late. She was carrying her lunchbox.

Suddenly J.J. felt as if he had a bunch of grasshoppers jumping around inside him. There wasn't much space on the lunchbox shelf. Ginny would have to move some lunches so she could put hers away. He swallowed hard and looked at Tanya. Tanya was already heading for the back of the room.

It was too late.

*CRASH!*

# It's Not Fair!

Ginny and Tanya yelled and jumped out of the way. Cans rolled everywhere. Some went up the aisles between the desks. A sardine can stopped right by Kyle's foot. He kicked it away and climbed on top of his desk to get away from the smell.

Everyone was laughing, except J.J. and Tanya. Their faces were bright red.

Miss Davis stood up. "All right," she said in a quiet voice. She was really mad. "Who did this?" She looked at J.J. and then at Tanya.

At recess time, when the other kids lined up to go outside, J.J. and Tanya each got several sheets of paper, their pens and some Superwhite. They went to sit in the hall.

"This is going to take forever!" Tanya said.

"Think I don't already know that?" J.J. knew better. It would take longer than forever. Writing *I am not a detective. The teachers will solve the problem.* One hundred times. With no mistakes. By tomorrow morning.

Already J.J.'s hand was beginning to ache. Tanya looked over and pointed out some mistakes. J.J. groaned and reached for the Superwhite.

He didn't pay attention when somebody walked by. All he saw was a pair of blue running shoes and legs in dirty grey jogging pants.

Tanya jabbed J.J. with her elbow. "Who was that?"

"Quit jiggling me!" J.J. said. "See what you made me do?" He jabbed Tanya back.

And then the fire alarm went off.

J.J. grabbed his paper and pen and raced out. Let Tanya worry about the Superwhite!

Outside, the kids were lining up in their usual places. But the teachers looked confused.

"I smell smoke!" Ginny Chen said to somebody as J.J. went by.

As usual, Shaun was goofing around in line. "School's burning," he said with his crazy laugh. He bumped into J.J., knocking the papers out of his hands.

"*Shaun Higgins!*" Mr. Muller thundered. "Come here and stand with me."

Shaun gave him an "I don't care" look and went to the head of the line. On the way, he walked all over J.J.'s lines. He left big muddy footprints across the writing.

"Hey!" J.J. yelled. "You wrecked my lines!"

Tanya got into line behind J.J. "I saw somebody!" she said. "You know the kid who walked past when we were writing? He went into a classroom!"

"Quiet, Tanya," said Miss Davis. She took hold of Tanya's elbow and led her to the front of the line.

"Think I care?" J.J. muttered to no one in particular.

He stood there feeling mad as the teachers checked attendance. Maybe there really was a fire. Fire drills never lasted this long. At last the bell rang and they went back inside. J.J. crumpled his messed-up lines and tossed them into the garbage as he walked past. "Think I care?" he said again.

At lunchtime, J.J. started writing even before he opened his lunchbox. But he was too hungry to work on his lines for long. He opened his lunchbox — and yelled. The criminal had struck again.

"It's not fair!" J.J. said when he took his lunchbox to show Mr. Muller. "*Twice!* Why does he always have to pick on me?"

But J.J.'s lunch wasn't the only one taken this time. In all, ten lunches had been stolen. Tanya's was missing. So was Ginny Chen's. And several in other classes.

The only good thing about it, J.J. decided,

was that Shaun's lunch was missing too.

They all went to sit in the nurse's office with Mrs. Markoski while Miss Davis went out to buy lunch for everyone.

"We saw the criminal," Tanya said in an important voice. "He had light brown hair, a dirty blue T-shirt and grey jogging pants."

"And blue running shoes," J.J. added.

Mrs. Markoski looked puzzled. "You're absolutely certain?" she asked.

"He was going into the classrooms!" Tanya said. "After the fire alarm went."

Mrs. Markoski looked around. "Does anybody here know anything about why the fire alarm went off today?"

Silence.

"There was no fire drill planned," she said. "If anybody here knows anything about it, I want to know. Now."

Suddenly J.J. had an idea. He looked at Tanya. "The criminal!" he said. "I bet he made the alarm go off —"

"— so he could get more lunches," Tanya finished up.

Mrs. Markoski's mouth tightened. But before she had a chance to say anything else, the door opened. Miss Davis walked in carrying two big bags.

J.J.'s mouth watered at the smell. Hamburgers! He was so hungry he could hardly wait.

"Wish I could get my lunch stolen every day," Shaun said. "This sure beats peanut butter." He poked J.J. with an elbow and grinned. Surprised, J.J. smiled back.

Miss Davis handed him one of the warm hamburgers and J.J. began unwrapping it. But before he could take a bite, Tanya jabbed him in the ribs.

"Get it?" she said. "Nobody was missing from the fire drill. That means somebody else is coming into the school and stealing our lunches!"

# More Things Go Wrong

"**Y**ou think you're so smart. So solve the problem yourself!" J.J. yelled into the telephone that evening.

He slammed the phone down. He was sick of the lunchbox mystery. He was sick of Tanya. Now she was even calling him at home! And he still had to write 69 more lines. *I am not a detective. The teachers will solve the problem.* Yes, let the teachers solve the problem. Or let Tanya do it. He didn't care anymore.

Mom was busy working on a big project for one of her classes. Jessica was crying in her playpen. J.J. decided to drive his Z-28. It zoomed past the refrigerator and shot under the table. Oops! It crashed into a chair leg. The batteries fell out and rolled across the floor.

"J.J.," his mom called. "Please! Can't you keep quiet while I'm studying? Why don't you go play in your room until supper time?"

"When are we eating?" he asked. It was past 6:00. As far as he could tell, nothing was cooking.

"Oh, dear," she said. "I haven't even thought about it."

"I can make hot dogs in the microwave."

"Would you, J.J.?" Mom appeared in the doorway holding Jessica. "You're an angel."

J.J. didn't want to be an angel, but he did want supper. He thought of saying that if he fixed supper maybe Mom could do some lines for him. But he decided he'd better not.

Mom put Jessica back in her playpen and she started crying again.

"Can't we make her stop?" asked J.J.

"I wish," said Mom. Suddenly she was

talking to him as if he were a grownup. That felt kind of good.

"Maybe she's hungry," J.J. suggested.

"Of course!" cried Mom. "I missed her afternoon snack."

You missed mine too, thought J.J. But he didn't say it. He said instead, "The lunchbox criminal stole my lunch again — and other kids' lunches too. So Miss Davis bought hamburgers for everybody."

"Would you mind giving Jessica some cheese and a cut-up apple?" Mom asked.

"Hey!" said J.J. "I said, my lunch —" Then he stopped. Mom wasn't listening.

He sighed and cut up some cheese and an apple. He dropped the pieces into the playpen. Jessica laughed and crawled over to get them. He could smell her messy diaper. But there was no way he was going to take care of *that!*

While he waited for the microwave to buzz, he wrote a few lines. He even wrote between bites while they ate.

That was a terrible mistake. Jessica decided to throw her plate. It was full of cut-up pieces of hot dog, strained carrots and applesauce. The whole plate landed right on top of J.J.'s lines. Upside down.

J.J. felt like tipping over the high chair. "Now I'll have to do them all over again!"

Mom hugged him and wiped the carrots and applesauce off his lines. Then the phone rang and she went to answer it. J.J. put his head down on the table.

"That was Miss Davis," Mom said when she came back to the table. "She says you don't need to write any more lines. She says the teachers and the principal are all going to work hard to solve the problem of the stolen lunches."

"Oh," said J.J. He was glad that he didn't have to finish the lines. But he was disappointed too. Why couldn't he and Derek — and Tanya, he guessed — solve the mystery on their own?

# A Closer Look at the Criminal

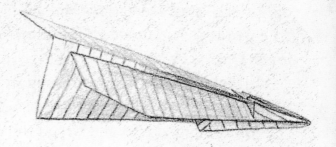

By the next morning J.J. had figured out what they had to do. He and Derek and Tanya would have to race the teachers to see who could solve the mystery first. He was trying to explain this to the others as the class lined up for an assembly. But too many other kids were talking.

"I think the assembly's about bicycle safety," Ginny Chen said.

"I bet it's about tricycle safety," Kyle said.

"Remember the jugglers we saw last time?" said Michael Strongchild. "They were good!"

"We've got to race the teachers!" J.J. said to Derek for the third time.

"Huh," said Derek loudly.

"Quiet down, class!" Miss Davis sounded kind of tired. "We aren't going anywhere until it's so quiet we can hear a pin drop."

"What kind of pin?" asked Kyle. "A bowling pin?"

Miss Davis gave Kyle a look that made him extra quiet.

"We have to race the teachers!" J.J. said again.

"Oh, I get it!" Tanya said. "To see who —"

"*Class!* If you don't quiet down right now, you won't be having gym today."

Suddenly it was quiet. *Very* quiet.

J.J. thought he saw the lunchbox criminal again as they were going into the assembly. He was walking along with Ms Eaton-Cook's class. When he got closer, he recognized the hair, the jogging pants, the runners and the dirty T-shirt.

Nobody else knew the lunchbox criminal was there, not even Derek. J.J. stared hard at the boy's back. That was the geek who'd stolen his lunch — not once but twice. What could he do? It had to be something that wouldn't get him in trouble. And he'd have to do it quickly. Ms Eaton-Cook's class was just about to go into the gym. What was the criminal going to do, sit through assembly just like every other kid? Wouldn't people notice him?

J.J. had an idea as they were passing the bulletin board. Lots of notices were stapled to the board. He tore one off and folded it into a paper airplane. He aimed it at the criminal's back. He didn't miss.

The criminal turned around. It was a girl!

J.J. was so surprised that he forgot to walk when the line started moving again. How could the criminal be a girl? But he was sure he wasn't mistaken. When he looked again, she was gone.

The assembly was long and boring. Mrs. Markoski talked a lot about the stolen lunches. J.J. kept turning his head, trying to see if the criminal was in the gym. Miss Davis finally pulled him out to the aisle and gave him a talking to. He didn't really listen.

Was the criminal in the gym? What would she think, hearing herself talked about in front of the whole school? J.J. was sure she wouldn't like it!

No lunches were missing that day. It was almost disappointing. And because tomorrow was Saturday, J.J. knew he'd have to wait until Monday to do anything.

# Dead Meat

When he'd finished watching cartoons the next morning, J.J. went down to the river to meet Derek. In the distance, he could see Tanya delivering flyers. And there was Amy, jumping rope like always.

After finding out that the criminal was a girl, Tanya had been even more interested in solving the mystery. But J.J. didn't feel like talking to her right now. He pushed through the branches. A mosquito kept whining in his ear. He swatted it. Branches scratched his bare arms. Derek was late, as usual.

Suddenly, J.J. heard a rustling in the

hideout. "Why didn't you tell me you were here already? I've been waiting half the —"

"Whatcha doing, ratface?"

*Shaun!* J.J. backed out as fast as he could. This was total disaster! If Shaun knew their hideout, they were dead meat!

Branches swayed wildly as Shaun came after him. "Nobody invades my fort and gets away with it!" he yelled.

Once he was on open ground, J.J. took a deep breath. "It's not your fort! We found it first."

"It is now," Shaun said. His foot wrapped around J.J.'s ankle and J.J. landed hard on his chin. He said some bad words as he got up.

But Shaun just laughed. He pushed and caught J.J. off balance. J.J. staggered. He slid down the bank toward the river.

And then he heard a familiar yell. There was Tanya, advancing toward Shaun.

"Stay out of this, Tanya," J.J. yelled. "This is between Shaun and me!"

She ignored him and kept on coming. When she got close, Shaun kicked out at her. But she wasn't quite where Shaun expected her to be. There was another yell and Shaun went flying. He landed like a sack of scrap metal. Tanya sat on him.

"I saw what you did, you bully!" she screamed at him. "You'll pay."

J.J. laughed. He started back up the bank so he'd have a better view. But then Shaun wriggled free. He scrambled to his feet and caught Tanya in a headlock. "Think you can mess with me?" he said. He tightened his grip and Tanya started choking.

J.J. broke into a run. He'd have to do something or Tanya might get hurt.

Suddenly he was in the middle of a tangle of arms and legs. Something hit him in the nose and blood ran down his shirt. He saw Shaun's face right in front of him and punched wildly.

"You kids!"

The voice sounded far away, but J.J. knew he'd been hearing it for a while. It was Mrs. Peterson. He saw a hand clamp down on the back of Shaun's neck. Then something yanked him backwards too.

"You kids!" Mrs. Peterson shouted again. "Always fighting. At this rate you'll land in jail before you get out of grade school."

"He started it!" J.J. yelled. Mrs. Peterson's grip on his neck felt like iron. His bottom lip was starting to swell up like a balloon. He licked it. It tasted like blood.

Mrs. Peterson didn't seem to care who had started it. But she let go of them. "Your parents are going to hear about this," she said.

J.J. groaned. Now he wouldn't be able to sneak inside and clean up. When Mom saw him like this, he'd be sent to his room for the rest of his life! Or at least until it was time to get Dad at the airport.

J.J.'s mom *was* angry, but not quite the way he expected. She dropped her books onto a chair and her mouth went into a hard line. She sent J.J. upstairs to the bathroom to wash his face and change his shirt. When he came down again, she was sitting by the telephone. Jessica was crying in the playpen.

"Where does Shaun live?" Mom asked.

"Angus Crescent," J.J. said. "Why?" He stared in surprise at his mother. What was she going to do, march over to see Shaun's mom and beat *her* up?

But Mom opened the telephone book instead. She told J.J. to take Jessica for a walk in the stroller.

"Do I have to?"

"Go," his mom said in her "do not argue with me" voice. He did as he was told.

# A Big Break

**J.J.** hadn't gone very far when he heard running footsteps behind him.

"J.J.! Wait!" It was Derek.

J.J. kept going, but a moment later Derek had caught up. "What happened to your face?" asked Derek.

J.J. frowned. "What happened to your *hair?*" he asked. Derek had been to the barbershop, he could see.

"Is that why you took so long? I waited and you never showed up. Shaun was in our hideout."

"That geek!" cried Derek. "We'll have to get him for that."

"I already did," J.J. told him. "I pounded him." J.J. was starting to enjoy himself. He made his fat lip stick out a little farther.

Derek looked impressed.

"Hey! Guys!" It was Tanya calling them.

"Oh, no!" said J.J.

Just then Jessica threw her rattle onto Mr. MacDonald's lawn. The sprinkler was going.

"Jessica!" J.J. snapped. He knew that if he just left the rattle there, he'd get in trouble. So he darted into the sprinkler and got his clean shirt wet.

"Guys! *Wait!*"

Darn! Tanya had caught up with them. Worse yet, little Amy wasn't far behind. Her jump rope was trailing along the sidewalk. Tanya had a place on her cheek that looked pretty sore.

"We really got *him*," she said.

"Huh?" said Derek. "Got who?"

"Shaun," Tanya said.

"*Huh?*"

"My mom's phoning his mom right now," J.J. added, to change the subject.

"What happened?" asked Derek.

"I *told* you," J.J. said. "You wouldn't have missed it if you hadn't been a hundred years late."

But Tanya started telling Derek all about it.

Jessica was babbling. "Hi, little baby," Amy said as she blew a big bubble of gum. Jessica grabbed for the big pink bubble. It popped all over Amy's face and stuck to Jessica's fingers.

"*Jessica!*" said J.J. But he couldn't help laughing, even though it made his face hurt.

"Serves you right, Amy," said Tanya. "Always showing off with your gum."

"I don't care," Amy said. "Gillian blows bubbles all the time."

"Who's Gillian?" J.J. asked.

"It's her imaginary friend," said Tanya. "She says this kid lives in the school and eats lunch with her."

"She's not imaginary!" Amy cried. "She's real. She doesn't have any home and —"

"Oh, sure," said Tanya. "Go jump rope, Amy. OK?"

J.J. glanced at Jessica. She was watching a ladybug crawl on the back of her hand. Then, without warning, she popped it into her mouth.

J.J. didn't know what to do. Were ladybugs poisonous? What if Jessica died and it was all his fault? "I better get Mom," he said.

"It won't hurt her," Tanya said. "I remember when Amy ate a fly."

"Ughhh!" said Derek. "I think I'm going to be sick."

J.J. felt the same way. "Are you sure?" he asked, looking hard at Tanya.

"Would I lie? Of course I'm sure," she replied.

"Gillian said she swallowed a mosquito once," Amy said.

"Can't you be quiet? We're not interested in imaginary friends," Tanya said.

Amy stamped her foot. Gum was still stuck to her nose.

"How many times do I have to tell you?" she yelled, getting red in the face. "Gillian's not imaginary. She lives in the school with her big sister and her sister gets lunches . . ." Amy put both hands over her mouth as if she'd just done something awful.

Suddenly it was very quiet.

"The criminal!" J.J. gasped.

"Oh!" said Tanya and Derek at the same instant.

"Our first big break in the case!" said J.J.

"No!" cried Amy. "Don't tell! I'll get in trouble! Gillian will get in trouble! Roxanne will be really mad." She looked very little and very scared. "Don't tell!" she begged again. "I promised not to —"

"You just *un*-promised," Tanya said in a bossy big-sister voice. "I'll give you all my packs of bubble gum if you help us."

"No," said Amy. "How many packs do you have?"

"Three," said Tanya.

Amy shook her head. "No. I can't get Gillian in trouble."

"I'll buy you some gum," Derek said.

Jessica squealed and drooled. J.J. wiped her chin. The ladybug had not come out. At a time like this, why did he have to take care of his baby sister?

"We'll buy you five packs," Tanya said. "And ten red licorice."

Amy shook her head again.

"Can't you just help us?" J.J. asked. "Please? I'm tired of getting my lunch stolen."

"Me too," Tanya agreed. "It's not fair to all the other kids at school either."

"But they all have homes," Amy said. "And moms who give them food. And clothes."

"What?" said Tanya. She looked at J.J. and Derek, then back at her little sister. "This sounds serious. You'd better tell us — or I'll tell Mom and then she'll tell Mrs. Markoski."

Amy got very quiet.

"I'll buy you a Barbie," Tanya went on. "With my own money."

Amy got even quieter. "They ran away," she said in a tiny voice. "Because their dad went away and didn't come back. And their grandma got sick and went into the hospital."

J.J. took a deep breath. One or two missing lunches was nothing compared with *that*.

"What about their mom?" he asked. "Why doesn't she help?"

"She died," said Amy. "A long time ago."

"Oh," Tanya said in a quiet voice.

Amy started crying.

"Don't worry," Tanya said. "We'll help them. We *have* to. But how?"

# Meeting the Criminal

When J.J.'s dad got home that night they all went out for dinner. While they were eating, J.J. asked what happened to kids who had no homes. His dad talked about social workers and foster parents. It sounded awfully scary to J.J.

By Monday morning J.J.'s fat lip had gone down, but Shaun had a black eye. He walked around with his head down and didn't bug anybody much.

As they were lining up, Tanya came rushing over to them. Amy was following her. And a little girl in dirty clothes was following Amy.

"This is Gillian," Tanya said. "She says she'll help us talk to Roxanne."

"We brought extra lunches today," Amy said. "Tanya made them and Mom didn't even notice."

J.J. looked at Gillian. She was skinny and looked scared. He wondered if she really would get in trouble for telling the secret. "We'll meet at recess," he said. "Behind the tunnels."

It seemed to take forever for recess to come. J.J. kept wondering where Roxanne was. How could she and Gillian live in the school? Did they sleep on the cots in the nurse's office? How come nobody had caught them?

"J.J." Miss Davis said. "Can you tell us the name of the hot liquid inside the earth that makes volcanoes?"

"Huh?" J.J. gulped. All around him hands were waving in the air.

"I know!" cried Tanya. "It's —"

"Magma!" J.J. said loudly.

"Thank you, J.J.," Miss Davis said. "I thought maybe you weren't listening."

J.J. grinned.

How were they going to get Roxanne to come talk to them? Maybe they could pretend to kidnap Gillian and take her to the tunnels and Roxanne would see and follow them.

"J.J."

Miss Davis again! "Huh?" He was beginning to sound like Derek.

"Would you care to come get the papers for your row?"

J.J. felt his face getting hot. How did Miss Davis know when he wasn't paying attention? She seemed to catch him every time.

"I have a plan!" he whispered as he passed Derek's desk. Across the aisle, Tanya listened.

Amy and Gillian were already jumping rope by the time J.J. and the others got outside at recess. J.J. grabbed Amy's rope and ran. Amy yelled and chased after him. Behind him he could hear more yells and several sets of running footsteps. He hoped Mrs. Hoff, the yard-duty teacher, hadn't noticed. Crouching behind the concrete tunnels, he waited. Derek appeared. Then Tanya and the two little girls. "Shh!" said J.J. He held a finger to his lips. They waited.

One more set of footsteps came pounding toward them. An angry face peered around the tunnels and glared at them. "Hey! What are you doing to my little sister?" Roxanne looked so mean that J.J. gulped. She looked even meaner than Shaun!

"It's OK," said Gillian.

"Are you kidding?"

J.J. took another deep breath. "We know about the lunches," he said. "We know what happened."

Roxanne grabbed Gillian's wrist. "Did you tell? I thought I could trust you!" She started dragging her sister off toward the fence. "I *told* you —"

Tanya started talking fast. "We want to help. We brought more food for you."

"We don't need your help," Roxanne said.

But Tanya wouldn't give up. She started talking again. She asked where they were from. She told them how brave they were for doing what they'd done.

Roxanne didn't want to talk. "We're from Winnipeg," she said at last. "We're going to my aunt's. She lives somewhere near Vancouver."

"But how — ?"

"We took the bus," Gillian said shyly. "Roxanne saved money from shovelling snow and cleaning people's yards. But there was only enough to buy tickets to Regina."

"We brought you extra food," Tanya said. Roxanne's chin began to quiver and her eyes suddenly looked watery. She turned away. Gillian ran over to hug her sister.

Then the bell rang.

J.J. didn't feel like going back inside. But he could see Mrs. Markoski standing there

with the yard-duty teacher. "You should tell a grownup," he said. "They'll help."

Roxanne's chin jutted out. "We don't need anybody," she said.

But Gillian's face crumpled. She started to cry.

"Oh, great," sighed Derek. "And we're going to be late too."

J.J. knew what he had to do. "I'm going to tell," he said. "So people can help you find your aunt."

Without warning, Roxanne punched him in the stomach. He staggered backwards. Then Roxanne grabbed Gillian's hand and yanked. "Run! They'll call the cops!"

But Mrs. Markoski had seen them. And Gillian wouldn't run. Instead, she just stood there looking at Amy, J.J., Tanya and Derek.

J.J. had to catch his breath. Mrs. Hoff was calling for them to come inside. J.J. walked toward her, but backwards. That way he could watch as the principal talked to the two girls.

"Wow!" said Tanya. "Can you imagine doing all that? Saving money to buy bus tickets and then living in a *school?*"

"Anybody could do that," Derek said.

But J.J. wondered. He was having trouble imagining what it would be like not to have any house or food — or parents to take care of you. Then his heel bumped against the step. It was time to go inside.

Derek turned to J.J. "Hey!" he said. "I guess we solved the mystery, huh?"

"Right," J.J. agreed. But it hadn't turned out quite the way he'd expected. Two homeless and hungry girls . . .

"I solved it too."

J.J. had forgotten all about Amy. But there she was, tagging along as usual.

"Huh," said Derek.

"She did," J.J. said before Tanya could get mad at him.

"Come on!" Mrs. Hoff called. "You're late, all of you."

# Some Answers

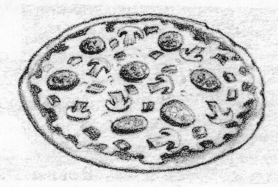

J.J. couldn't figure out what to do at recess the next morning. After spending all that time trying to solve a mystery, the idea of just playing seemed kind of boring. Besides, he kept wondering what was happening to Roxanne and Gillian.

"Look at Shaun," Tanya said, laughing. "He still has a black eye."

"I know," said J.J. He almost felt sorry for the bully. It couldn't be much fun walking around school with everybody staring at you. "I wish we knew what's going to happen to the criminal," he said.

"Roxanne," Tanya corrected. "Me too. I hope they find their aunt. Wouldn't it be awful if they couldn't?"

"We're going to miss the excitement," Derek said sadly.

"Unless we find another mystery!" Tanya's eyes sparkled.

"No way!" said J.J. Maybe, without any mysteries, Tanya would get bored and go play with some girls. But it *had* been kind of fun.

"Are we in trouble again?" Derek asked suddenly.

J.J. looked up. Mrs. Markoski was walking toward them.

"We didn't do anything this time," said Tanya. "We can't possibly be in trouble."

But J.J.'s heart started beating in a scared way.

"I thought the three of you might like to hear the news," the principal said. "The Children's Aid people have found Gillian and Roxanne's aunt and she's on her way right now. She's been worried. She wants to take the girls home to live with her."

"Oh, good!" said Tanya.

J.J. felt a warm, quiet happiness. "I'm glad they're going to be OK," he said. It just wasn't fair for kids to have it so rough. He thought of his own family. He had a mom and dad who loved him — even baby Jessica wasn't so bad. He felt lucky.

Mrs. Markoski walked away and the bell rang.

"We really helped them!" Tanya kept saying as they went to line up.

"I know," said Derek. "We heard you the first time."

J.J. was backing away from Tanya when he bumped against somebody else. It was Shaun.

The old fear J.J. usually felt when Shaun was around was gone! Shaun moved away without a word. Kyle was right behind him. He gave J.J. and Tanya a strange look — almost as if he was scared of *them!*

J.J. laughed suddenly and jabbed Tanya in the ribs.

"Ow!" she yelled. "Quit it!"

J.J. shook his head and walked into the school. His stomach was growling. It was going to be a long wait until lunch. But at least from now on he could be sure of finding a full lunchbox.

As he walked into the classroom, J.J. checked the shelf, just to make sure. His lunchbox wasn't there!

"Hey!" he said. "Somebody stole my —" And then he remembered. His lunchbox was still sitting on top of the TV. He'd been in such a hurry to leave for school that morning he'd forgotten it.

"Oh, no," he groaned. "And it was pizza too!"

7